Katharine Tynan

Miracle Plays

our Lord's coming and childhood

Katharine Tynan

Miracle Plays
our Lord's coming and childhood

ISBN/EAN: 9783337367848

Printed in Europe, USA, Canada, Australia, Japan

Cover: Foto ©Andreas Hilbeck / pixelio.de

More available books at **www.hansebooks.com**

OUR LORD'S COMING AND CHILDHOOD

SIX MIRACLE PLAYS

MIRACLE·PLAYS : OUR· LORDS·COMING·AND CHILDHOOD

ET·VERBUM·CARO·FACTUM EST

BY · KATHARINE · TYNAN · HINKSON ·

CHICAGO : STONE·AND·KIMBALL·
CAXTON· BUILDING ·
LONDON : JOHN · LANE ·THE·BODLEY·HEAD·
MDCCCXCV·

TO THE REV. T. DAWSON, O.M.I.

CONTENTS

ILLUSTRATIONS

BY PATTEN WILSON

Before I tell of thee, God's Son,
And all the sweet salvation
That Thy birth brought to labouring men.
Make me Thy little child again.
Bid me put off the years, and be
Once more in meek humility
Thy little one and wondering-eyed.
Give me their faith who stood beside
The manger that Thy cradle was;
Vision of oxen and of ass
To see Thee curled on Mary's knee.
Yea, give me their humility.
Give me the quiet heart in breast,
And pure eye of the kindly beast
That gave its meal to be Thy bed,
And so was greatly honoured.
Ere I behold Thy mysteries
Force Thou my soul upon her knees.

THE ANNUNCIATION

Lilies in our garden
    Take the light, pure and white;
Lilies in the moonlight
    Like a silver flame.
Lilies in our garden
    Shed perfumes, all a-bloom.
Bearing then a white lily
    Blessed Gabriel came.

Silver-pale his lily
    Like a sword flashed and stirred;
Scimitar of Heaven,
    To lay Satan low.
Shining like his lily
    Mary went, sweet, content,
Walking in her garden
    Flower of gold and snow.

Heaven hath no lily
    That with her can compare.
Lily for God's bosom,
    At the break of day
Dreaming in her garden,
    Pure and fine, crystalline.
For us, mournful sinners,
    Maid Mary, pray!

Yet my heart ached to hear the noise
They used to make, my two dead boys;
There was the shelf with all their toys
          Put from my aching sight.

I hungered for the toil they made,
When in my door there came a shade
Or light perhaps, I unafraid,
          Looked up and saw his grace.

And shading then mine eyes did speak,
Though all the glory made me weak:
Great Lord, what is it that you seek
          In this unworthy place?

First Woman
What answered he?

Second Woman
                    Most sweet and fair,
He said: I am a wayfarer
By fields of earth and fields of air,
          Sad mother, and no Lord.

I turned and set a chair, and laid
Before him wine and wheaten bread,
And cherries white and cherries red
          And water in a gourd.

First Woman
Did he partake?

Second Woman
                    He drank; and gave
His thanks, as sweet as when you lave
Tired feet within the sparkling wave,
          So fell they on my heart.

Then asked he me where lived the man
Joachim, and his good wife Anne,
And took his lily and staff again,
  And blessing, did depart.

Third Woman (entereth)
Say, have ye seen him?   As I came
Up from the well, weary and lame,
One with the amber hair like flame
  Dazzled, and passed me by.

There was a sudden burst of song,
And bells in heaven pealed loud and long;
What marvels while the day is young
  Are wrought in earth and sky?

How he was clad I know not.   Eyes
That saw that Bird of Paradise
In plumage all of gold and price,
  Still ache from that fine sight.

Since he hath passed my foot hath rest;
The sick child crying on my breast
Sleeps like a young bird in the nest,
  And all the world is light.

Who was he?

First Woman
    Rachel here can say.
His foot was on her floor of clay;
(That floor belike was blest to-day);
  His hand was on her head.

Second Woman
I only know what he did seem.
He sought our neighbour Joachim;
But what his embassy with him
  The great lord has not said.

Third Woman

Our neighbour Joachim he hath
The fairest child in Nazareth,
A lily snatched from sin and death,
    Mary, his tender girl.

At evening in her garden close
She tends her lily and her rose,
Sweetest where many a sweet thing
  blows,
    A pure and perfect pearl.

First Woman

Dove's eyes are hers, and the dove's
  heart,
And lips whence words of kindness start,
Lonely and lovely, set apart
    For some most favoured lot.

A living lily that our God
Tends in a garden off the road
Where never a foot of man hath trod,
    And evil weeds spring not.

Second Woman

What if some king from over seas
Hath heard what pearl of price she is,
And here hath sent his embassies
    Entreating her sweet hand?

Then would he take and set her on
A burning diamond for her throne
And weave the stars to make her crown
    In his most splendid land.

PATTEN WILSON

[SCENE II.—MARY'S bower. She sitteth alone spin-
ning. By her side is a lily in flower. Outside the casement a bird in green vines singeth.]

Mary

I would I might praise perfectly
Like lily of mine, and wind and bee,
And like my bird that sings to me,
    The Lord of earth and heaven.

I but a young maid am, and do
My father's will and mother's too,
Have naught to choose and naught to rue
    From golden morn till even.

I sing and spin, I pray and weave,
And watch my lilies bud and leave,
And hear my birds sing in the eave,
    And ever muse upon

The Child that will one day be born
To lift our hapless world from scorn;
For all our race sad and forlorn
    To win salvation.

I never see a babe at rest
Upon some village mother's breast,
But mine eyes seek in anxious quest
    If that sweet Babe be He.

I pray that in my time may rise,
That Babe for whom my heart hath eyes.
That I may ere my last breath sighs
    That Rose of Sharon see.

I would I might be handmaiden
Unto His mother. Blessed then
To sweep and cleanse of soil and stain
    The house for that fair Boy.

The An= Perchance, His mother would Him lay
nuncia= Once in mine arms, on some sweet day
tion When she was sudden called away.
   Then should I die of joy.

  Meanwhile God sends me friends. They
   come
  In troops at twilight to my room,
  They sit and help me at my loom
    And set the purple threads.

  Whereof I fashion without seam,
  A purple garment in a dream,
  Very lovely my strange guests gleam
    With shining wings and head.

  If I might make His baby-clothes
  Softer and silkier than a rose!
  Happy is she who sits and sows
    His robe of linen fine.

  Or who shall wash His clothes; and
   make
  The bed where He His rest shall take.
  O Babe, for whom my heart doth ache,
    Sweet Star, arise and shine!

    [The ANGEL floats in mid-air.]

The Angel
Hail Mary!

Mary
    Who art thou to come
In such strange splendour to my room?
Brethren of thine do haunt my loom,
   Yet those by thee were dim.

18

The Angel

Hail, Full of Grace!   Blessed art thou
Among all women.   With thee now
The Lord is.   He before whom bow
      Seraphim, Cherubim.

Mary

I fear.   What dost thou seek of me?

The Angel

Fear not! The Lord has honoured thee,
Thou shalt conceive and mother be
      Of a most Holy Son.

And Jesus thou shalt call His Name.
He shall be great and of great fame,
Son of the Highest; and the same
      Shall reign on David's throne.

His Power and Kingdom shall not end,
Power of the Highest shall descend,
The Holy Ghost shall hover and bend
      Above thee, Blessed Maid.

Mary

Behold the handmaid of the Lord!
Be it according to His Word.
Now come, Thou great and golden Bird!
      No more am I afraid.

She said, Thy will be done,
And, lo ! the Holy One
    Took life within her breast.
The trembling Heart of Love
Began to throb and move
    Where Love had built His nest.

When many years were gone
He said, Thy will be done,
    And, lo ! His Passion-Hour
Broke on the world's black night;
The long-desired dawn-light
    Oped like a rose-red flower.

Sweet Mother and sweet Son,
Who with, Thy will be done,
    Fulfilled the Father's will,
Give to our hearts to say
Ever, although He slay,
    His will be blessed still !

THE VISITATION

Though all unmeet for that,
   Let us draw nigh to hear
Mary's Magnificat,
   Tender and without fear.

Worthless, and flawed, and small,
   Yet let us cry and swell
Her praise angelical,
   Who praiseth Thee right well.

THE VISITATION

[SCENE I.—The Inner Sanctuary of the Temple. Outside a great multitude prayeth; within the blessed ZACHARY kneeleth and swingeth a censer.]

Zachary

FLOAT clouds and wreathe the feet
    of Him
Who sitteth on the cherubim
Whose hair hath made the noontide dim,
        Whose face warm splendours veil.

Bear Him our praise, that worlds away,
Worship Him from our hearts of clay;
And pray Him take reproach away
        Wherewith the world grows pale.

Years come and go. The world's womb
    bears
Myriads of men, sad labourers,
Whose groans are heavy in His ears:
        And yet there tarrieth

The Sun of Righteousness that shall
Lift from the world her heavy pall,
And bid us stand rejoicing all,
        Escaped from living death.

Blessed their seed from whom shall
    spring
The great Deliverer and the King,
Yea, and our sin's burnt-offering
        For whom the nations pray!

And blessed He who biddeth come
The barren and the fruitful womb,
And some hath filled right full and some
    Hath empty sent away.

[THE ANGEL appeareth standing at the right hand of
the altar of incense.]

Zacbary

I fear thee, Angel of the Lord,
Thine armour and thy flaming sword.
Winged art thou like the golden bird
    That holds His mysteries.

Leave me, who dare not even behold,
Thy shoon of diamond and of gold!
What dost thou do with me, grown old
    And empty and unwise?

The Angel

Fear not! Thy prayer hath reached
  the Throne,
Elizabeth shall bear a son,
The which his name thou shalt call John,
    And he will bring great joy.

Not only unto thee grown gray
And her, so patient many a day,
Whose long reproach is taken away.
    But to the world, this boy.

He shall be great in the Lord's sight.
Wine nor strong drink shall him delight.
The Holy Ghost shall fill him quite
    Even from his mother's breast.

And he shall make the Lord his road,
And turn the children's hearts to God,
And like Elias walk abroad
    With power and spirit blest.

28

Zachary

How shall we know these tidings dear?
For we are old this many a year.
So long the Lord delayed to hear,
  Our last sweet hope is dead.

The Angel

Gabriel am I, who stand before
The Presence, while the heavens adore
And gold wings sweep the golden floor
  And many a golden head.

Gabriel am I, His messenger,
His Archangel trusty and dear.
And mine the greatest Word to bear,
  To men who toil and die.

But since to hear me thou art slow,
Be dumb until these things be so.
And by this token thou shalt know
  The Lord hath heard thy cry.

[SCENE II.—At the door of ZACHARY, his house,
MARY lighteth down from the ass which JOSEPH lead-
eth. All below stretch plain and river.]

Mary

Thanks, little ass, who did me bear
To this hill-country, blest and fair,
And a more precious wayfarer
  Than thou canst understand.

Blessed be thou, O patient one,
For kindest service kindly done
To me and my most royal Son,
The King of many a land.

Joseph

Art tired, my dearest? Here is peace
In this white house 'mid apple-trees,

29

Where thou canst rest and take thine
ease.
>   A land of honey and milk.

See, then, how far below the plain,
The river but a silver stain
That windeth in and out again,
>   A ribbon all of silk.

Mary

How thick the grape-vine groweth o'er
My cousin, Zachary, his door.
'Twere sweet to sit an hour or more,
>   And taste the purple vine,

Here on this bench. Although in truth
The Father of my Babe made smooth
My way, and many a gold-haired youth
>   Served me with milk and wine.

[ELIZABETH appeareth in the doorway coming to
welcome them. Of a sudden she is seized with a tremor
and falleth at MARY'S feet.]

Elizabeth

Blessed art thou, so kind to come
And visit my unworthy home !
The child hath leapt within my womb
>   Hailing thy Holy One.

Blessed art thou, tender and young,
Blessed art thou women among.
Thou bearest Whom saints foretold and
>   sung.
>   Blessed thy blessed Son.

Mary (raiseth her hands to heaven)

Magnificat anima mea Dominum.
Et exultavit spiritus meus in Deo Salutari meo.
Quia respexit humilitatem ancillæ suæ; ecce enim
>   ex hoc beatem me dicent omnes generationes.

Quia fecit mihi magna qui potens est; et sanctum nomen ejus.
Et misericordia ejus a progenie in progenies
timentibus eum.
Fecit potentiam in brachio suo; dispersit superbos
mente cordis sui.
Deposuit potentes de sede et exaltavit humiles.
Esurientes implevit bonis et divites dimisit inanes.
Suscepit Israel puerum suum recordatus miseri-
cordiæ suæ.
Sicut locutus est ad patres nostros Abraham, et
semini ejus in sœcula.

Elizabeth
Now am I highly honoured.
Thy table will I gladly spread,
And bring thee milk and whitest bread,
And wash thy tender feet:

And while thou bidest with me, will be
Thy handmaiden most reverently.
The Lord look on this house and me,
And make us worthy, sweet.

Mary
Dear cousin, I am come to stay
Three months upon thy happy way,
To help thee at thy work, and pray,
And talk with thee upon

What God hath done for us, and praise
His Name. And sweet the happy days
With household tasks in this sweet
place,
And thy son and my Son.

At morning we will bake and brew,
And dust and sweep each morn anew,
And gather berries cool with dew,
And in the afternoon

31

Will sew our baby-clothes, and kiss
The cloth where his sweet limbs and His
Shall curl, more softly than the rose is
  That openeth in June.

[Turneth to her spouse.]

Here's Joseph then.   He hath put up
Our ass and given him bite and sup.
He now will gladly taste thy cup,
  And share thy fruit and bread.

And afterwards wilt take us where
Thy garden hangs in scented air?
But here the Lord seems everywhere,
  Heaven is so close o'erhead.

She is come with tender speed
All to help a woman's need.

She has brought that house within,
Folded up in leaves of green,

Rose of Sharon, that shall bud
To a Rose as red as blood.

Maid and mother, turn with speed
To all women in their need.

Turn to all who travail sore,
Light and comfort in the door.

Bring Thy Son with thee and rest
While their need is heaviest.

THE NATIVITY

The fold at midnight
  Was light as the noon,
And in a tree a birdie bright
  Sang still the gladdest tune.

With wings of gold sheen,
  And gold head and hood,
He was the fairest bird, I ween,
  That ever sang in wood.

He sang sweet and low,
  He sang loud and shrill ;
Above the stable in the snow,
  The Star stood still.

The shepherd swains said then—
  Each fell on his knee—
That was the very sweetest strain
  Was ever sung in tree.

Are many birds in bower
  With many a dulcet song;
But none like him who sang that hour
  The Christmas boughs among.

God's Way of Giving

'Twere bliss to see one lark
Soar in the azure dark,
Singing upon his high celestial road,
I have seen many hundred soar, thank God !

To see one spring begin
In her first heavenly green
Were grace unmeet for any mortal-clod,
I have seen many springs, thank God !

After the lark the swallow,
Blackbirds in the hill and hollow,
Thrushes and nightingales, all roads I trod,
As though one bird were not enough, thank God !

Not one flower, but a rout,
All exquisite, are out ;
All white and golden every stretch of sod,
As though one flower were not enough, thank God

—Katharine Ty

THE NATIVITY

[SCENE I.—Shepherds on a hillside, watching their flocks by night.]

First Shepherd

THE frost is crackling in the grass:
   'Twere well the flock warm-housed
      was.
How merrily now the time would pass
   Were I by mine own fire.

Second Shepherd

Ay, neighbour, sad the shepherd's lot.
Whether the wind be cold or not,
He must away from wife and cot,
   To frozen field and byre.

First Shepherd

Where's Jacob?

Second Shepherd

   See! he cometh now
Yonder, over the wheatfield brow;
And in his arms he hath, I trow,
   A young lamb, newly born.

Let's heap the fire; the wind brings snow;
And feed the little life that's low;
Lamb's life and babe's life flickering go
   In this gray hour ere morn.

Third Shepherd (entering, a lamb in his arms)
Brothers, a little lamb I bring,
A curled and soft and helpless thing;
Its mother died at birth-giving;
        And see the blood upon

The fleece! as though one marked it thus
For sacrifice most piteous.
There's room enough for this with us,
        Beside my little son.

First Shepherd
Brothers, the night grows still and fair,
What balmy warmth is in the air?
Look ye, whence comes that splendid
    Star,
        Travelling to Bethlehem?

Third Shepherd
To-night some marvels we shall see.
Golden-clad folk went down by me,
All shimmering from the head to knee,
        Each with a diadem.

Second Shepherd
Peace now! For see above our hill
The heavens are opening wide, until
The golden glory bids us kneel
        And praise God in the night.

See, rows on rows of shining ones,
All chanting, in their silver tones,
Matins and Lauds and Orisons,
        In one long golden flight!

The Angels Singing
Gloria in Excelsis Deo,
Et in terra pax hominibus
Bonæ voluntatis!

First Shepherd

Lo! they are hushed; but flutes begin
A silver music, soft and thin.
In one long trail the stars move in
        And lean above the town.

'Tis the stars singing that we hear,
Like silver trumpets ringing clear.
How purely floats each silver sphere.
        We too will travel down.

All

Come up, come up, black fleece and white,
Wether and ewe, and lamb so light,
And you, the wean was born to-night,
        Come follow the Star's track!

It beckons us the way it goes,
And Tib, our dog, the creature knows,
He too, in bitter frosts and snows,
        Saw Gates of Heaven rolled back.

(They gather up their belongings, and all go out.)

[SCENE II.—The stable. Mary sitteth in the grass of
the manger, the BABE on her knee. JOSEPH kneeleth
by her. The ox and the ass mildly gaze upon her and her
SON.]

Mary

Sweet Son, and is it thus you come
To such a poor, unworthy home?
Better than this was Mary's womb,
        Unworthy though it were.

Nine months have I desired you, sweet,
To kiss your prisoned hands and feet,
But never dreamt your face to greet
        In a sad stable, bare.

Sleep, little one, sleep sweet, mine own!
Mother shall rock her dearest one.

To-night He is her own, her Son,
    Whatever the years bring.

In Nazareth she hath laid by
Great store of baby napery,
With lavender sweet and rosemary,
    All for her Baby King.

Joseph
Mary, give me His feet to kiss.
Alack, that in such a place as this
The Child is born, Whom on my knees
    Most humbly I adore.

Thou knowest how through this cold-
  heart town,
Weary, I travelled up and down,
Praying a shelter for mine own,
    All in her need so sore.

There was no woman, sweet, to come
And take thy hand, and lead thee home,
And find the hours not wearisome,
    To watch by thee till morn;

And with a woman's art to soothe
The Holy Babe, and wash and clothe.
Great glory they have lost, in truth,
    By their cold hearts of scorn.

Mary
Come hither, little ox and ass,
That gave my Son your scented grass;
His Hand shall o'er your foreheads pass
    In love and thanksgiving!

What would we do, both He and I,
Had ye the cold world's cruelty,

Shelter and cradle to deny
     To this most Holy Thing?
       (The Ass and Ox kneel down.)

Now bless them, little Baby Son,
Thy wrath for their oppression;
Thy blessing when there's kindness
   done
     To these who gave Thee bed.

Yea, blessed these so wistful-eyed
That watched Thy bed of birth beside,
And heard Thee when Thy dear voice
   cried,
     And saw Thee clothed and fed.

O little ass and ox, in truth
Great glory shall accrue to both,
For when the cold world lay in sloth
     Ye kept the watch with joy.

And by your breath the frosts were
   thawed,
Your kind brown eyes saw and were
   awed;
King of the world, the angels' God,
     And mine own new-born Boy.

Joseph
Now, by the golden light of stars,
And the great crown each angel wears,
I see a throng of wayfarers.
     Coming across the moor

Are shepherd men, and men like kings,
And every one his present brings;
The sheep, the shepherds' shepherdings,
     And dog, are at our door.
    (Kings and Shepherds enter and kneel.)

Melchior

We are three kings from farthest Ind,
Travelled these many weeks to find
The greatest King of all mankind.
    And since the Star hath shown

That this most precious Babe is He,
We worship Him on bended knee,
With silk and spice of Araby,
    And gold to build His throne.

I, Melchior am, old beyond man,
Ages ago my reign began;
Now to this Babe of scarce a span
    I kneel, and kiss His feet.

Dear King, Thou sweet and tender One,
Linen I bring Thee finely spun,
And cloth of gold for Mary's Son,
    To be His garb unmeet.

Caspar

Widowed of love, I frozen-eyed,
Since the black grave had snatched my
    bride,
Watching one night pavilions wide
    Of stars in a dark field,

Saw one Star ruddier than a rose;
And by my palace casement close
Heard a great voice: The way it goes
    Follow: thy wounds are healed.

Yea, we have followed patiently.
Thou gentle Babe, now take from me
Sendal and spice from over sea,
    And frankincense and myrrh.

And I, too, kiss Thy tender feet,   The
Where the red blood doth pulse and beat, Nativ=
Making a stain both dark and sweet,   ity
  As though a nail went there.

Balthazar
I, young, with all the world before,
Glory, and love, and power in store,
Kneeling most humbly, I adore
  The Babe in swaddling clothes.

The Star to me sang clear, there was
Here in the manger and the grass,
A King whose greatness did surpass
  All that a mortal knows.

Sweet little Child, the gold I bring
Is an unworthy offering.
But would that for my kingliest King
  A palace I might build,

With hall, and tower, and shining stair
All of the gold and ivory fair,
And million windows in the air
  That the late sunsets gild.

First Shepherd
Hail Thou Whom the Star heralded
Comely and tender in Thy bed.
Lady, I bring to His Godhead,
  Being but a little Child,

A bunch of cherries, smooth and ripe,
Likewise a shepherd's oaten pipe;
He laughs whilst thou the tears dost
 wipe,
To see my cherries wild.

45

Second Shepherd

Hail, Sovereign Saviour, Who hast
    sought
Us, by Thy seeking brought to naught,
Wilt take a little bird I caught,
      That hath a tuneful throat?

Sweetest of sweetings, happy this
That Thou shouldst greet it with a kiss,
And in Thy sweet hand make its bliss,
      And chirrup to its note.

Third Shepherd

Hail, dearest dear, full of Godhead,
Be with me in mine utmost need.
A lack, to see Thee in such weed
      Of pleasant things forlorn!

Behold, I bring thee but a ball,
The which a child finds good withal.
Hail, Holy King, asleep in stall,
      Of Whom the world hath scorn!

Mary

Kind gentlefolk, who came to seek
My little Son, new-born and weak;
I thank you, since He cannot speak,
      And lift his hand to bless,

At in-going and out-coming
And on your homeward wayfaring,
And wife and wean and everything
      Ye hold in tenderness:

Be free from woe, where'er ye go,
Kind gentlefolk, that honour so
The Babe that came in frost and snow.
      He bids ye go in peace.

To Kings and kindly shepherd men,
And dog, and sheep that turn again,
Of His sweet countenance full fain,
    Be health and full increase.

The Angels Singing

Laudamus te, benedicimus te, adoramus
  te,

Glorificamus te.   Gratias agimus tibi
Propter magnam gloriam tuam.

There lay the Baby King,
  Holy and undefiled ;
The earth can show no sweeter thing
  Than a little child.

A flower is fine and sweet,
  And sweet is a bird,
But sweeter far from head to feet
  Was the Baby Lord.

A lamb is very meek,
  And pure is a dove ;
The Lamb of God was small and weak,
  All purity above.

Most blessed was she
  Who had Him for her own ;
Who rocked Him on her tender knee,
  Whose bosom was His throne.

Right blessed she was
  Who fed Him at her breast,
And while the nine sweet months did pass
  Made for Him a nest.

THE PRESENTATION IN THE TEMPLE

For Him was offered up
  A pair of doves, whose harmless veins
Should brim His sacrificial cup
  And wash away His stains.

His stains, withouten spot,
  All golden pure from head to feet;
The doves in binding meshes caught,
  Of Him were emblems meet.

Yea, for His mother's blame
  In bearing Him, the doves were given,
O thou who takest away Eve's shame,
  And openest gates of heaven:

Is 't thus thou comest, sweet,
  So lowly with thy glories dim ?
They cannot see from head to feet—
  God's light wraps thee and Him.

THE PRESENTATION IN THE TEMPLE

[SCENE I.—Outside the gates of the Temple. On the Temple steps are seated mendicants, etc. A group of women of all ranks waiting. MARY entereth with the CHILD in her arms, and JOSEPH, who carrieth two doves. They wait at the outskirts of the crowd.]

Mary

HERE seemeth now a goodly throng:
    I pray our waiting be not long,
Lest that the Babe, not over-strong,
    Should suffer and repine.

I praise His Father with full voice,
And with my sisters here rejoice,—
All joy be with these mothers of boys
    Who have a joy like mine!

Joseph

Art thou not tired? The doves wilt take,
And I the Child? He will not wake.
Thou'lt see what careful nurse I make —
    I shall not let Him fall.

Mary

Nay, Joseph; for we lightlier go
Than thy sweet pigeons winged with snow.
I would He might be ever so,
    Nor leave mine arms at all.

The Presen-tation in the Temple

Sad is it for the mother when
Her babies grow to fearless men,
And never can be small again,
    And she their moon and sun.

But the child wakes. My sweeting, see
Babies like Thee, but none like Thee,
Of high degree and low degree,
    And cheerful every one.

And yonder, little Lamb, behold,
A white ass and his gear of gold.
I would my Baby, five weeks old,
    On such an one might ride.

And see Thy doves! Each pretty neck
Shot with the rose and purple streak,
But snowy wings without a fleck,
    And wee feet, scarlet-dyed.

[A woman approacheth with a curtsey, and speaketh.]

Lady, thy Baby is so fair,
Such waves of glory on His hair,
We, mothers of many babes, aver
    Was never such a child.

Second Woman

Such babe as this the Prophets saw
Foreshadowed in our ancient law.
Tender He is, yet full of awe,
    A Lamb all undefiled.

First Woman

He seems to bless our babes and us
With His dear smile and gracious.
A sweeter smile than babies use,
    He hath, this lovely Thing.

O hands like rosebuds crumpled close,
And little feet like any rose,
O Rose that in the winter blows,
  Of all the roses King!

[The Temple doors open. As they pass in, a beggar toucheth his sores to MARY'S gown and is healed. He standeth in the sunlight praising GOD.]

Joseph (loquitur)
Marvels are all about thy path,
Rose in the world of sin and death;
Blessed the man whose eye seeth
  Mother and Baby blest!

Yea, blessed I, who have for spouse
This Lily with the silver brows.
And her sweet Son within mine house,
  My foster-Son and Guest!

Meek and obedient hath she been,
Since by the winding ways of green
I led her home, and brought her in
  Across my threshold poor.

No child is simpler than this Maid
And Mother. Awe makes me afraid
To see her bake our daily bread,
  And wash, and sweep our floor.

No common household task, not one,
Is there that she hath left undone.
So many linen webs hath spun,
  So many simples brewed.

Our house is sweet with sunlit air,
Wherein God lays His secrets bare,
And works His marvels past compare
  From day to day renewed.

[SCENE II.—The Temple. The other women are filing through distant door. SIMEON waiteth by the altar. ANNA THE PROPHETESS on her knees prayeth. MARY advanceth, holding the CHILD on her outstretched arms.]

Simeon

Who is it? Speak, for I am blind
And old and tired, and yet designed
To see great things before the wind
    Of death hath blown me out.

O in my dark the glory grows,
  And on my heart the rapture flows,
Like his, who sees at last and knows,
    God's light his head about.

Speak! Is the time come? I should stay,
Yea, even to the eternal day,
Though all the planets withered away,
    Until my Star was risen.

My Star that breaks through night and
  gloom,
And through the darkness of the tomb,
And to my sightless eyes is come
    As to the souls in prison.

Mary

This is Babe Jesus, small and fair:
And I the Mother did Him bear,
Spouse of Joseph the carpenter;
    Of Nazareth are we.

And here I offer, holy priest,
These pretty doves with irised breast,
That he and I may be released,
    And of the birth-stain free.

[She placeth the BABE in SIMEON'S arms.]

Simeon (lifteth his sightless eyes)

Nunc dimittis servum tuum,   Domine, secundum
verbum tuum in pace.
Quia viderunt oculi mei salutare tuum.   Quod
parasti ante faciem omnium populorum,
Lumen ad revelationem Gentium, et gloriam plebis
tuæ Israel.

Anna

This I have waited for is come,
And it is time I were gone home,
Full threescore years since on a tomb
    My widow's tears were shed.

I prayed my dim eyes should not close
In death's sweet silence and repose,
Till on the world's thick darkness rose
    The Star of the Godhead.

Glory to Him who heard my prayer.
To Child and Mother did Him bear.
Mary, spouse of the carpenter,
    Be praised in prayer and song.

In whom the great Light woke and grew,
Of whom world's hope was born anew,
From whose sweet breast the Baby drew
    The milk to make Him strong.

Simeon

This Child is set for rise and fall
Of many an one in Israel all;
A sign they speak against withal
    When many years are past.

Yea, thine own heart the sword shall ope,
Thou mournful Mother of our Hope.
So may the many hearts yield up
    Their secrets at the last.

59

Mary

Thy words are dark, thou holy man;
Yet swift and sudden the swords ran
Piercing my heart.   The pain began
    Upon thy prophecy,

Of some dark day when One must die.
O very dimly I descry
Three crosses under a maddened sky:
    All else is hid from me.

Come, little Lamb, there is sweet peace
At home beneath our cherry trees,
And dappled skies of blue and fleece
    From whence the sweet airs fall;

And arbors where a little one
Might shelter from the noonday sun;
And alleys green where he might run
    When he would play at ball.

Sleep, little Bird; sleep sweet, my Dove,
In Mother's arms and Mother's love.
From Nazareth we shall not rove,
    My little Boy and I.

In Nazareth angels' wings brood o'er
With angels kneeling by our door,
And feet of angels on our floor,
    And swords of angels nigh.

Let us go home; for home is best,
Child Jesus! where love builds Thy nest,
And none can harm Thee, loveliest,
    Except Thy Father will.

On Him in trust my cares I lay,
For this and for a distant day.
Be His to save or His to slay,—
    Blessed His Name be still!

The blind old priest of sacrifice,
Lifting to Heaven his sightless eyes,
Praised God that unto him was given
To hold the Baby new from Heaven,
Child - King of earth and Paradise.

To that meek, trembling Mother-Maid,
What were the words of woe he said ?
O little Sword of God, that went
Through her kind heart and innocent;
Thus was her mother-love repaid.

THE FLIGHT INTO EGYPT

The false gods from their place fell down,
  And they were broken, one and all,
When there came to the Egyptian town
  Mother and Baby fair and small.

In from the desert where long syne
  Thou soughtest for me, come speedily,
My walled town, closed to trump of thine,
  Opens unto Thy baby cry.

See, the false gods are on their face,
  Broken to pieces altogether ;
My soul is as a desert place,
  Yet come, dear Child from wind and weather.

THE FLIGHT INTO EGYPT

[SCENE I.—JOSEPH sleepeth in a room white with moonlight. Outside Bethlehem lieth still in the morn. JOSEPH dreameth and uttereth aloud his dream.]

Joseph

ARE they not safe? I heard, me-
   thought,
The crying of women sore distraught,
And through that lonely sound I caught
   The shriek of babes, and then

Clashing of swords, and oaths, and fierce
Wild laughter rang against mine ears.
Mine eyes beheld the dripping spears
   In hands of wicked men.

'Twas night in Bethlehem did seem
All through the horror of my dream.
And 'Woe!' and 'Woe to Bethlehem!'
   I heard a voice cry on.

And yet I know the small town lies
Soothed by the sweetest lullabies,
Watched by a million starry eyes
   That gaze until the dawn.

I know the babies lie at rest,
Each rosy on its mother's breast,
Wherein Love makes the tenderest nest.
   O hard-heart little town!

The Flight Into Egypt	That bade my Dearest in her need Take refuge in the cattle-shed, And gave her sweetest Son for bed The cattle's manger brown.

Nevertheless sleep well, and far
Away from thee those cries of war!
Sleep sweetly under the Birthnight Star
    Until the cock shall crow.

The while I list, as soft as love
The tender breathing of my Dove
And the dear Babe her heart above
    Breathing so soft and low.

[A radiance floated in his dream, in the midst of which appeareth THE ANGEL OF THE LORD.]

The Angel

Joseph, arise! no time for sleep
If thou thy trust with God wouldst keep.
Leave Bethlehem town to wail and weep,
    But thou, up and away!

Take Mother and Child, and ride in haste
Across the desert still and vast.
Saddle thine ass and ride thee fast,
    Be far ere break of day.

Herod now seeks the Child to kill,
Up and away with a good-will.
Soon will the winds of dawn blow chill,
    The day of blood be red.

Save thou the Child! Here will be moan,
Weeping and lamentation lone
The voice of Rachel for her son
    Mourning uncomforted.

[JOSEPH waketh and peereth in the moonlight. He then ariseth hastily and wakeneth MARY.]

Joseph

Dearest, rise up and take the Child,
We must away ere yon star mild
Wanes in the day. While yet He smiled
    In sleep, a vision rose,

And warned of danger dark, and death.
Wrap thee right warm. The morning
  breath
Is cold, and cold the night bloweth
    The way our journey goes.

Mary

Alas, and is it so soon they seek
To slay my Babe new-born and weak?
This little One so soft and meek
    No wild beast would Him harm.

Saddle the ass. We two will be
Ready by then to ride with thee.
My Sweet shall take no chill with me,
    My veil and cloak are warm.

Come, Little One, now leave behind
The town where we no roof could find
The night that Thou wast born. Unkind
    The desert need not prove.

For Thee to whom the world is ill,
Yea, raveneth like a wild beast still,
My white and innocent Lamb to kill,
    Come, tender little Dove!

    [They pass out into the darkness, where JOSEPH hold-
eth the stirrup-rein of the ass.]

[SCENE II.—In a robber's cave in the desert. MARY laveth the little JESUS in clear water, while by her side LEAH, the robber's wife, suckleth her babe.]

Leah (singeth)

Sleep sweet, my baby
　　Whiter than snows,
Rose of the desert
　　That in the night blows.
Round my wan rosebud
　　Floweth my veil,
Screening my white rose,
　　Tender and pale.

Little white rosebud,
　　Be not in haste
Yet to uncover
　　To the hot blast.
World's breath will scorn thee,
　　Cruel winds blow,
Ravage my rosebud
　　Whiter than snow.

Lullaby, my rosebud,
　　Grow not a rose ;
Round thee to shield thee
　　Mother's veil flows.
Rose of her darkness,
　　Make her heart glad—
The saddest poor mother
　　That ever earth had.

Mary

Why then, my sister, dost thou sing
So sad a cradle song to wing
Thy baby into slumbering ?
　　　Nay, sweet, thine eyes be dried.

Kiss his soft feet and feel but this,
Thou art a mother, with that bliss
Turning all carking care that is
　　　To happy joy and pride.

We take the joy and grief in one,
We mothers who have borne a son,
And would not wish our lot undone
    If it were else all woes.

But hold my Jesus, and let me
Thy pretty baby on my knee
Nurse for a little. I would see
    The face thou holdest so close.

Leah (weepeth)
Lady, ah now, you touch my wound.
Where is a sadder mother found
All the sad earth o'er and around?
    O lady, see my child,

White with the leprosy! I dare
Not touch your Boy's sweet face and hair
Lest that my finger-tips should bear
    Those seeds rank and defiled.

Mary
Alas, poor mother, was this why
Didst lay thy precious baby by,
And would not let my gaze come nigh
    His piteous little form?

Nay, give him me, and take my Sweet
That is all sound from head to feet,
The evil thing, I fear not it,
    It cannot do Him harm.

Give me thy son, I will him bathe
Here where my one Son bathed hath.
Great virtue hath He evil scathe
    And taint away to take.

[Holdeth the babe, swiftly unclothing him.]

71

Now in the water I thee lay.
My Baby's Father, take away
This baby's leprosy, I pray,
       Even for Thy sweet Son's sake!

[She raiseth the babe from the water, wholly cleansed, and layeth him rosy in his mother's lap.]

Mary

Here is thy Dimas. Lift thine eyes,
See how he sweet and rosy lies
That piteous was and food for sighs.
       Now, sister, praise the Lord!

Leab (falleth down)

I praise His Name, and thee He sent,
His angel and His instrument,
To work on me His good intent,
       And on my babe and bird.

Mary

Praise me not. But if thou wilt, praise
My Baby through thy length of days
And praise His Father who had grace
       And pity for thy need!

Thou, little Dimas, who art clean,
I have a vision of thy sin,
And of thy sorrow that wins in
       At last to Heaven indeed.

O little Dimas, round and smooth,
I see thee in thy lusty youth
Brought down to death and shame in
   truth;
       I see thee keeping tryst

In a most bitter day and hour
When men are mad and hell hath power,
High where the awful crosses tower,
    Keeping thy tryst with Christ.

Little Dimas, when all is done,
Side by side with my little Son,
Thou winnest in when Heaven is won,
    O happy little child!

Now sleep. And sleep, my Jesus small,
For little birds are sleeping all,
And shadows lengthen on the wall,
    And fades the daylight mild.

The little robber child was scaled
  With foulest leprosy:
Yet Thy sweet bath-water availed
  To cleanse and set him free.
      So cleanse Thou me!

High by Thy side the same was set
  That hour upon the Rood.
His brow like Thine had bloody sweat,
  His feet like thine ran blood
      Thou Dear and Good!

Because he turned before he died
  And yearned to Thee with cries,
Didst call him, blest one, by Thy side
  To enter Paradise.
      Call me likewise!

THE FINDING IN THE TEMPLE

Where wert Thou then from dawn to night?
From candle-light to candle-light?
And what Thy Father's business
That kept Thee from her fond embrace?
No answer comes to us at all.

And wast Thou rapt away a while
To greet in Heaven Thy Father's smile?
Or did Thy feet go up and down
Still seeking sinners through the town
From outer wall to outer wall?

Just once Thy Godhead didst reveal
While Thy sweet childish years did steal
Slow and fleet as a child's years go.
Subject to her who loved Thee so,
And kept thy sayings in her heart.

O years of mystery! when Thy feet
Strayed 'twixt the garden and the street:
When Thou didst make Thee carpenter
And this one's table, that one's chair
Didst fashion all with cunning art.

I would we had but one sweet tool
Of Thine—Thy plane, Thy bench, Thy rule!

THE FINDING IN THE TEMPLE

[SCENE I.—Where two roads meet, a day's journey from Jerusalem. A group of men waiting, among them the blessed JOSEPH. Approaching by one of the roads a band of women.]

First Man

H ere they come buzzing like the bees
   In summer in the sycamore trees,
With 'so folks say,' and 'an' you please,'
      The foolish woman's way.

Second Man

Though they come from the Passover,
I trow the chatter doth not spare
Kind neighbours here, kind neighbours
   there,
      With 'lack !' and 'well-a-day !'

Third Man

And yet, good gossips, who decry
Your wives and mine, tell how and why
Ye think no other dame comes nigh
      Your own when all is said.

First Man

Right ! Yet I see among the throng,
One who doth shine our wives among,
—I do the honest souls no wrong.—
      As a star in a bed

Of daisies. 'Tis that Mary sweet,
Hidden and draped from head to feet
In veils of holiness, yet meet
          For human joy and pain.

Second Man

Mary being with our wives would be
No gossip, incivility
Or rude discourse. So rare is she
          Like some sweet lofty strain.

Third Man

Now Joseph sees her full of grace.
He too hath lilies in his face;
They say he is of royal race :
          Right wondrous is their Son.

First Man

What buzz of marvels gathers now
Round little Jesus, whose white brow
Draweth earth's light to rest, I trow,
          Like golden thorns thereon ?

Mary (cometh saying in her heart)

Little one, little Son of mine,
Thy mother's heart doth ache and pine
From day's uprise to day's decline
          Wherein she hath not Thee.

These kindly women's praise (she saith)
Quickens her heart, quickens her breath.
Thy Father's blessing fall (she prayeth)
          On these that pleasure me.

Joseph (advanceth)

Thou hast been slow, my queen, but where

Tarries the Boy, a loiterer?
What thing of earth or thing of air
      Hath tempted Him to stray?

Is it that he chases as boys do
Red moth or dragonfly in blue,
Or gathers blackberries in dew
      A little down the way?

Mary (paleth)

Is He not then with thee? When last
I saw him to thy side he passed,
Where the roads met; the throng was vast
      That either way defiled.

And thou and I went different ways.
My heart hath drunk all day his praise
And ached all day to meet His gaze
      And thine. Where is the Child?

Joseph

Grow not so pale! He stays behind
With friends and kinsfolk, warm and kind,
We will retrace our paths to find
      How safe the path He keeps.

Nay, sweet, can anything of ill
Happen without His Father's will?
Whose hand is o'er His own Son still,
      Whose heart keeps watch nor
      sleeps.

The Finding in the Temple

Mary

Three days these hilly streets have known
My feet that bleed, have heard my groan.
The swords turn in my heart, like stone,
    That lies yet hath no rest.

O heart that broke when Simeon spake
His woeful words, again wilt break ?
Seven swords of grief for my Son's sake
    Have pierced His mother's breast.

Joseph (entereth)

No news at all, nothing at all !
But silence like a brazen wall,
And yet what ill could Him befall
    Whose path the angels throng ?

My hands have knocked at many a door,
My feet trod many a stranger floor.
(I would not that she knew how sore
    My heart is.) Sweet, be strong !

Mary

I know His Passion draweth nigh
Ever and ever silently.
But day and hour that know not I.
    What if His Father's hour

Had struck ! And He, a child that lay
So warm, it seems but yesterday,
Betwixt my bosom and the hay,
    Were in His foes' dread power.

What if they racked Him at their will, The
And scourged His tender limbs until   Finding
They were one wound! What if they in the
  kill   Temple
        My Baby while we stay!

Or what if I unworthy proved
Had lost that precious charge beloved,
And He by angel hands removed,
        Were far and far away!

That were the least so it were well
With Him, dear friend, I scarce can tell
Mine anguish most intolerable,
        The fears that lurk and spring

And rend my soul like an ill beast.

Joseph
Come, in the Temple let us rest.
He will return to thy fond breast,
        As bird to mother's wing.

Come, where the lilies twine around
The marble fount, and silver sound
The waters: it is holy ground
        That dim, sequestered place.

Who knows if there we pray and kneel
His Father's counsel may reveal
What hiding-place doth well conceal
        The whole world's light and
        grace!

[They enter the Temple, where they behold the little
JESUS discussing in the midst of the doctors.]

The Finding in the Temple

Mary

Sweet Son, how hast Thou dealt with us?
So all unkind, unpiteous.
It was not like Thee to go thus
    And leave us to our fears.

Jesus

Sweet Mother, wherefore fears and woe?
Did ye not know I come and go
Upon My Father's business? lo!
    That calleth at mine ears.

First Doctor

Madam, is this thy Son? Then He,
This little Jesus, born of thee,
Hath all wisdom and prophecy
    Upon His childish tongue.

Second Doctor

A great prophet hath risen sure.
The Lord hath pity on the poor
And groaning world, and opes His door
    To send this seraph young.

Mary

Kind sirs, my Jesus, whom ye praise,
Is but a child in length of days,
Just such a little lad as plays
    At home about your knees.

For many and many a year to come
My little Jesus in our home
Will find the safety sweet, nor roam
    From where His mother is.

My little Boy beneath our rule
And at the kind dame's village school,
Will grow both tall and beautiful,
    And learn His father's trade.

I would not that by even a span
Ye clipped the child's days for the man,
Nor that too fast the dear years ran
    While yet my Jesus played.

Come, little Son, come home! Too soon
Thy morn will lengthen into noon.
About our eaves Thy blue doves croon,
    Thy kitten misses Thee.

And Thy small lamb that groweth big.
Thy garden-bed waits Thee to dig.
The bursting fruit on vine and fig
    Tempts now the honey-bee.

   [With salutations they go forth, the little JESUS holding His MOTHER'S hand.]

Because Thou wentest mourning
  Those three days up and down
The stony streets and burning
  Of that gray Eastern town,
And on the hilly street
Thy heart bled with thy feet.

Because within the Temple
  Thy joy went on before.
Thy little Son and simple
  Who taught the wise His lore,
Took then thy hand and went
Home with thee well-content.

Remember all souls roaming,
  Souls sick and sad and sore
Who pray not for His coming
  His feet upon their floor.
Take thou their hands and lead
Them home, aye home indeed!

Of my temerity
  Jesu, assoil me!
That I have dared to write,
  In all sincerity,
Tidings an angel might
  Tell of a verity,
With a pen steeped in light.
  Of my temerity
  Jesu, assoil me !

www.ingramcontent.com/pod-product-compliance
Lightning Source LLC
Chambersburg PA
CBHW032151010726
47493CB00008BA/2654